Fergus and the Princess

Malachy Doyle

Illustrated by Debbie Mourtzios

Rigby

Contents

CHAPTER ONE

The Closest of Friends

MANY years ago, in the land of green fields and swollen rivers, there was a king with a beautiful daughter. The little girl had golden red curls and sparkling eyes, and the king was more proud of his only child than he was of all his land and wealth.

Everywhere he went, his princess went with him, and the people would line the roadside with gifts of flowers. They all loved the child, yet they felt sorry for her as well. Her mother had died when the princess was born, leaving the king with a broken heart.

Often, the little princess would rise early and wander into the gardens to hear the blackbirds sing. One day, as she swung open the castle's great wooden door, she saw a small, dark figure hurrying away into the trees. A bundle of rags lay on the step. Looking closely, the princess found it was a tiny baby, wrapped in a blanket, fast asleep.

"Nanny, Nanny, come and see," she called, running inside.

"Oh, the poor, wee thing," said Nanny, carrying the baby back into the warmth of the kitchen.

2

Although the king's men searched far and wide, they never found the baby's mother. The princess named him Fergus, and from that day on, he was brought up as her brother.

Little Fergus grew into a laughing boy, and the princess into a beautiful young woman, with long, red hair and skin as soft as an apricot. Although there were eight years between them, they were the closest of friends.

Whenever the princess was happy, she and Fergus would laugh and run together through the long corridors of the castle of Dungannon, or in and out of the gardens. And whenever she was sad, Fergus could always cheer her up with his clowning and juggling.

CHAPTER TWO

The King's Fear

DAY by day, the princess grew more lovely, until the young men of Tyrone could not hide their admiration. The king began to grow fearful.

"You must not look at any of them," he told her. "No man is good enough for my daughter."

The princess loved her father and did as he said. But still the young men stared and the king grew even more fearful.

"You must cover your face," he told her. "They are not to see you."

From then on, every time they left the castle, the princess would tie a silken scarf around her head so that only her eyes were showing. And still the young men watched.

"You are to stay here in the castle," the king told her one day. "From now on, I ride alone."

The princess was very sad, for she loved to ride with her father on her fine, white horse through the rich farmlands of Tyrone, or deep into the hills and forests.

However, even with his princess safely at home in the castle, the king was not satisfied. For although he was the bravest of men, one fear stayed with him always. Ever since the death of his beloved queen, the king had been terrified that his daughter would one day fall in love and leave him forever.

"I have lost my queen," he told himself each night. "I could not bear to lose my princess."

Chapter Three

Locked in the Tower

The king gave orders for his soldiers to build a high tower in the middle of the Blackwater River close by.

For three months the soldiers worked and worked, and by the end of the summer they had built a great tower, fine and round, and higher than any in the kingdom.

The king rowed his daughter across the river to the tower, led her past the guard, and up the winding staircase. There were 500 steps, and at the top was the room in which she would live.

"Here, at last, you will be safe from the eyes of men," he said as he left. "I will visit you every day."

11

The princess wiped away a tear and looked around the room. The king had filled it with all her favorite things. Rich tapestries hung on the walls, and she had her harp, her paints, her sewing, as well as her table, chair, and bed.

She went to the window to watch her father row back to the castle, and she stayed to watch the sun go down over the distant mountains. Then she sat at her harp and played a sad but beautiful tune.

Early the next morning, the princess woke to the sound of oars splashing on the water. A new guard was coming on duty, but there was someone else in the boat with him—someone she was delighted to see.

Little Fergus ran all the way up the 500 steps and into her room. He put down the tray of food he'd brought, flew to the princess, and hugged her.

13

"My poor princess," said Fergus. "I'm so sorry for you, here all alone."

"Oh, Fergus," she said, "I was frightened that Father might not allow even you to come and see me. I don't know if I can bear it, locked away here like a prisoner. I shall miss my horse and my gardens so much. And who am I to talk to? Who am I to laugh with?"

"I'll come every day, Princess," said Fergus. "I can't bring your horse, but I can bring you your favorite flowers."

He revealed a spray of late summer roses. The princess held them tightly and breathed in their delicious scent.

"Oh, thank you," she said, smiling. "If each new day brings flowers and Fergus, I think I might survive."

Later that morning, the princess heard the sweet sound of a flute rising from the river below. When she listened closely, she was amazed to realize that the tune was the very same one she herself had played the night before.

Running to the window, she saw a small boat. In it sat a handsome fisherman, with skin as white as the first snows of winter, and hair as black as the raven.

To show her delight, the princess pulled some petals from her roses and tossed them into the air. They floated down on the breeze and landed all around the boat. The young man stopped playing, looked up at her, and smiled.

In the evening, the fisherman came back up the river, and once again, his melody filled the princess with joy. Again she scattered petals around him, and yet again he stopped to smile.

And so it was that the princess fell in love.

CHAPTER FOUR

Escape!

"OH, Fergus," the princess said one day when she couldn't keep her secret a moment longer, "I am in love with a simple fisherman and I must be with him. But I know Father will be in a terrible rage when he finds out. What am I to do?"

18

Fergus was frightened for her, but he promised to help in any way he could.

He remembered hearing of a wise old woman who lived in the woods of Benburb. He decided then and there to find her.

"Ah," said the old woman when at last Fergus arrived at her tiny cottage, "we meet again, young Fergus. What a fine and handsome boy you've become. How can I help you?"

Fergus looked at her closely. She was small and bent, but with a warm and honest smile, and he felt he could trust her. Although he was sure he'd never met her before, she seemed to remind him of someone.

"Old woman," he said, "my princess must escape from the high tower to be with her fisherman if she is ever going to be happy. I don't know what to do."

The old woman went inside and rummaged around her mantelpiece. "Here is what you need, Fergus," she said, handing him a small brown pot. "Take these seeds, give them to the princess, and tell her to cast them to the wind."

"But how will that help?" asked Fergus. "Surely they'll just float away down the river!"

"Wait and see, Fergus," said the old woman. "Wait and see."

Fergus did as she told him. He brought the seeds to the princess, who leaned out of her window and tossed them high into the air.

They fell to the water, as Fergus thought they might, and were washed away. But one tiny seed was blown into a crack in the base of the tower where the mud had gathered, and it began to grow.

The next morning, the princess woke early. The room was filled with a wonderful smell, sweeter than bluebells, more delicate than violets. She looked up and gasped, for the window was framed in pretty pink flowers.

Jumping out of bed, she ran across the room to find that overnight the whole tower had become wrapped in a great thick trunk. It wound all the way up from the river and was covered in a mass of pink blossoms.

The familiar notes of her sweetheart's flute floated to her ears. Looking upriver, she saw that his boat had just rounded the bend. Without another thought, she climbed out of the window and down the vines. The thorns dug into her body and tore at her dress, but she held on bravely and reached the bottom just as the boat rowed past. Letting go, she jumped, landing safely in the arms of her fisherman.

"Hide yourself in this, my love," he said, wrapping his coat around her. "I shall row to the great lake. No one will find us there."

The guard, tired from being on duty all night, noticed too late what was happening. He called for them to stop but they ignored him. Only after the morning guard arrived to replace him did the king discover that the princess had escaped, and by then she and her sweetheart were far away.

CHAPTER FIVE

Captured!

BUT the king had the fastest boat in the land. He called together 12 of his strongest oarsmen, who rowed with all their might. By late morning, they had caught up with the princess and her poor fisherman.

The king's terrible anger caused the boats to rock and the whole river to swell. The runaways were taken back to the castle, where the fisherman was put in chains and thrown into the dungeon. The princess was returned to her tower, weeping, and the pink rose vines were hacked down.

"Do not cry, princess," said little Fergus each day when he came to visit, but nothing he could do would make her happy. His clowning and juggling couldn't make her smile. She wouldn't play her harp or sing. She showed no interest in either the flowers or the food he brought her. She simply lay on her bed or stood by her window, weeping.

The king still came to see her, but she refused to talk to him.

Fergus returned to the wise old woman. She was standing at the door of her cottage as though she was waiting for him.

"I know why you've returned, Fergus," said the old woman, handing him a second little brown pot. "Take this to the king. But be careful, for he might be angry."

"How will it help my princess?" asked Fergus. "What will I do?"

"Wait and see," said the old woman. "Wait and see."

Fergus did as he was told.

"Father," he said, "the princess is fading away! She'll die unless you allow her to be with her fisherman." He handed the king the pot and ran out of the room.

The king opened it and lifted out the tiny wooden carving that lay inside. It was of himself and his queen.

CHAPTER SIX

The Crystal

AT first the king was very angry, for he had ordered every image of his queen to be destroyed after her death. He could not bear to be reminded of her. But as he stared at the carving, he remembered the days when his heart was filled with love.

Suddenly he knew how cruel he was being to his beautiful daughter by not letting her be with the man she loved.

He called for Fergus again and asked him to go down to the deepest dungeons with the chief of guards to fetch the fisherman.

The cells were empty. There was no sign of the poor man anywhere. Puzzled, Fergus was about to leave, when he caught a glimpse of something sparkling on the floor. He scrambled around in the dark until he found a beautiful red crystal.

Fergus placed it in his pocket and went back to the king's chamber.

"The fisherman has gone," said the boy.

"Surely he has not escaped?" cried the king. "No one can escape from my dungeons!"

"No," said the guard. "It's not possible. My men have been watching all day and all night."

"This was on the floor," said Fergus, holding out the shining crystal.

But the king was too upset to notice. "He must be found," he said, "or my princess will die of a broken heart."

Fergus knew that the crystal somehow held the answer. The next day, he returned to the woods of Benburb and asked the wise old woman for her help once more.

"Show me the crystal," she said.

He placed the crystal in her palm, and she covered it tightly with the long, bony fingers of her other hand and began to sing. Fergus watched closely as her fingers began to glow red.

When she opened them, the crystal was gone, and in its place was a delicate little bowl, with hearts and flowers painted all around it.

"Take this back with you to the castle," she said, handing it to him. "Put warm milk and honey in it and take it to the princess."

"How will it help her?" asked Fergus. "What will happen?"

"Wait and see, Fergus," said the old woman. "Wait and see."

CHAPTER SEVEN

A Secret Revealed

Fergus did as the wise old woman said. He returned to the castle, warmed the milk and honey, and poured it into the bowl. To his great surprise, he heard the sad sound of a flute coming from the bowl. He looked into the swirling heat, and for a second he thought he could make out the face of the fisherman.

Fergus dashed to his boat, rowed across to the tower, ran up the 500 steps, and pushed the bowl into the hands of the heartbroken princess, who was standing by the window, weeping.

"Drink!" he said, handing her the bowl. "You must, Princess, please!"

The princess was too weak and tired to argue. Without even glancing at the bowl, she took it in her hands and sipped. Then she, too, heard the music. She looked inside and saw the face of her beloved.

Tears poured from her eyes into the delicate bowl until it overflowed. The first drops trickled to the floor and suddenly, there where they fell, stood the fisherman.

In shock, the princess dropped the bowl, shattering it into a thousand pieces, and fell into the arms of the man she loved.

When the princess had recovered, the fisherman rowed them back to the castle where the king flung his arms around his daughter, delighted to see her smile once more. He threw his arms around Fergus, too, for bringing his daughter back to him. And then he hugged the fisherman.

"Please forgive me for how I have treated you," he told him. "If my daughter loves you and wants to be with you, then you are welcome into my family."

"Thank you, sir," said the fisherman. "I shall look after your beautiful princess all the days of my life."

The princess and the fisherman were married in the spring. The whole village of Tyrone came to the wedding. Fergus showered the bride and groom with rose petals.

In a quiet corner, two old women were whispering. One was the princess's nanny and the other was the wise old woman of Benburb, dressed all in black.

"Thank you for looking after my Fergus so well," said the wise old woman.

"Your Fergus?" asked Nanny, surprised.

"Oh, yes," she said. "I sent Fergus to the castle all those years ago to bring love back into the hearts of the king and the princess. And a splendid job he's done!"